Junction
NATHAN JUREVICIUS

Published by Koyama Press
koyamapress.com

First edition: September 2015

ISBN: 978-1-927668-21-4

Printed in China

Koyama Press gratefully acknowledges the Canada Council for the Arts for their support of our publishing program.

Junction
NATHAN JUREVICIUS

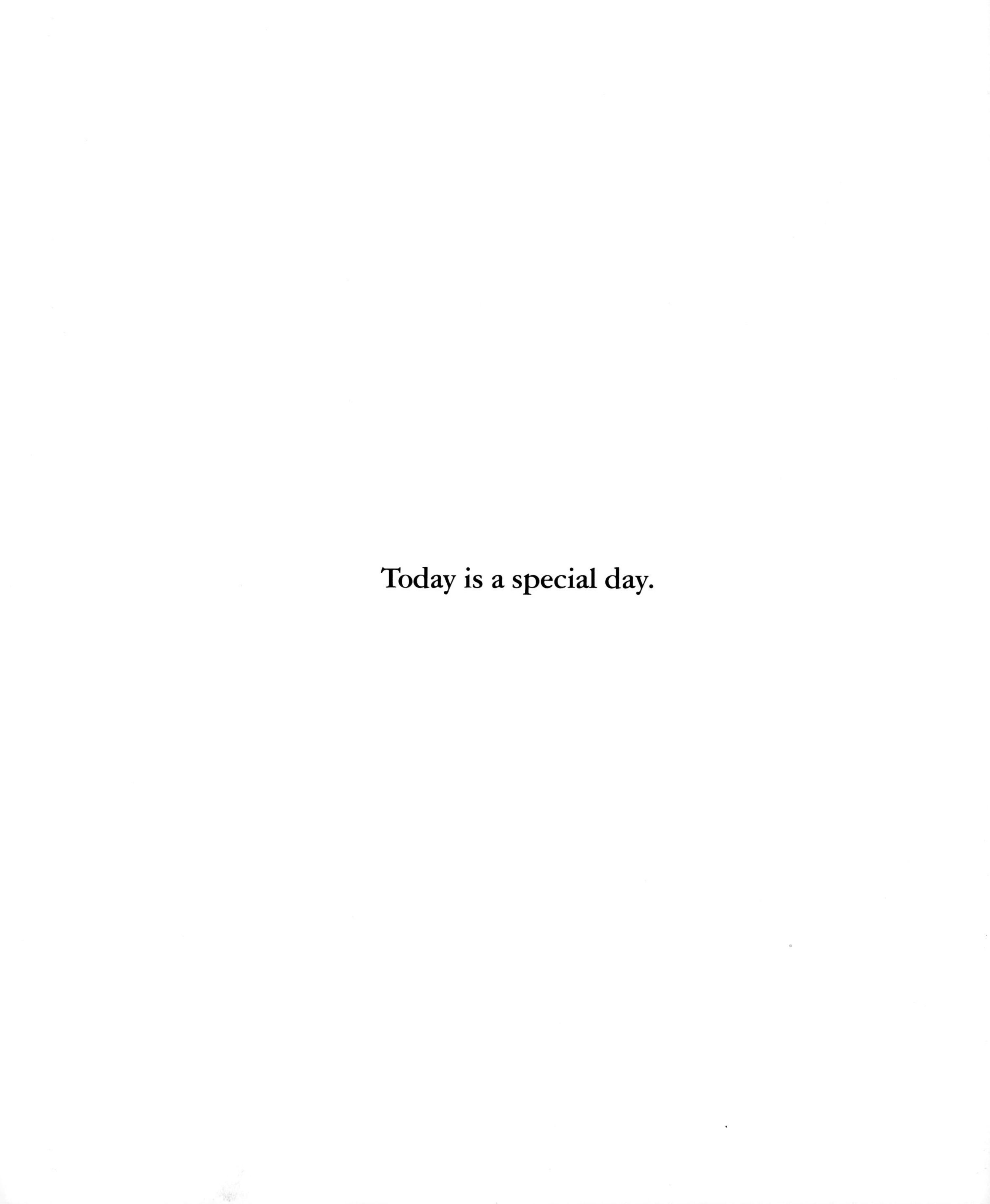

Today is a special day.

I feel excited...and nervous.

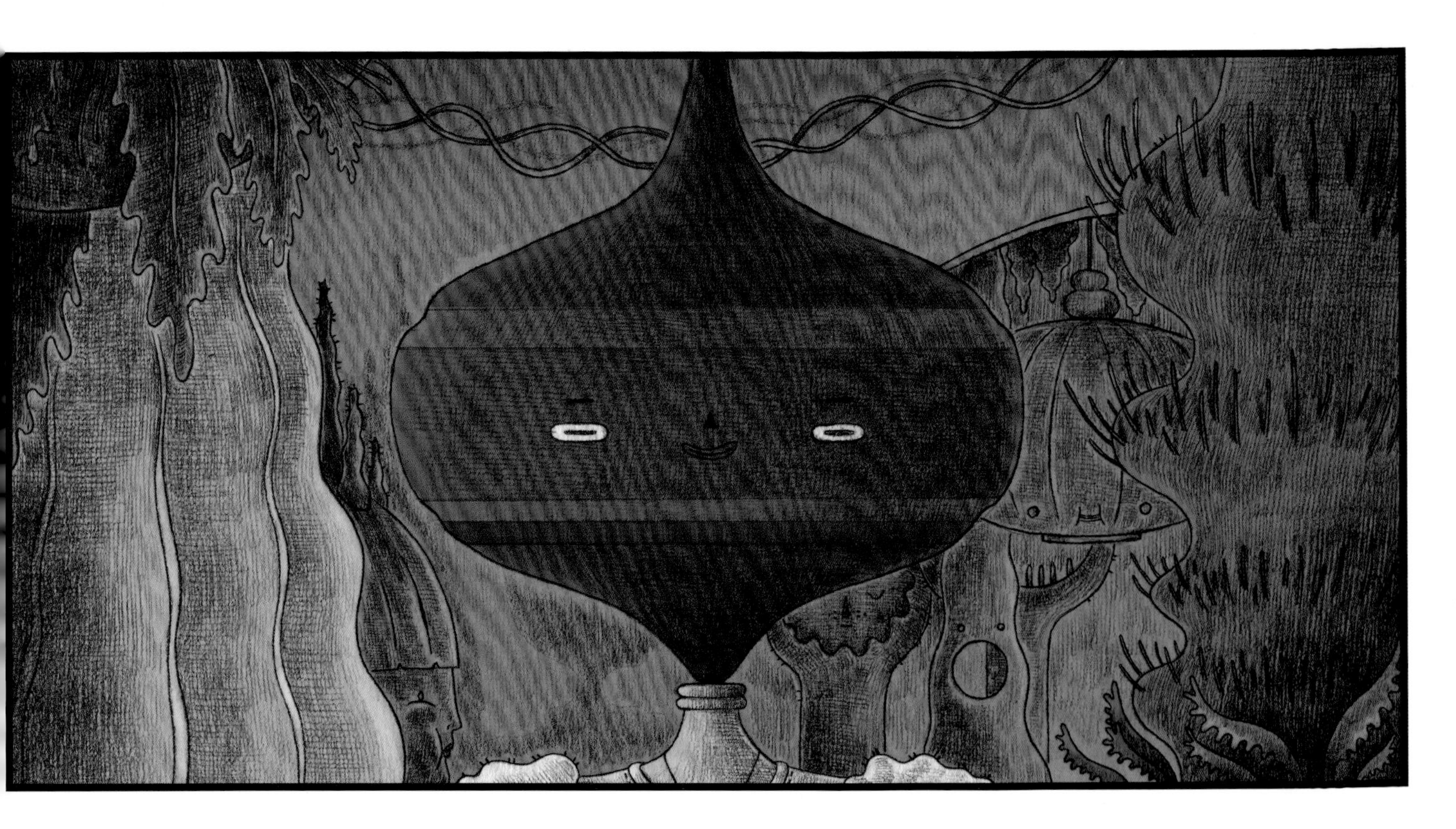

It's my turn to travel to the East Mountain — in fact, it's my first visit. I was old enough last year, but I broke my arm jumping from the roof of our house. My sister dared me to do it. I won the bet.

For generations my relatives have been the
Face Changers in this town.

It's a great honour, but I have to admit, sometimes it takes a
little getting used to when the transformation happens.

"A change is as good as a holiday" my grandmother always
says. I hope she's right.

I wonder what I'll look like this year?

An exotic plant? A ball of string? A crowded metropolis?

It's all a surprise!

I make my way
downstairs to the kitchen.

Every morning my family sits together and eats breakfast.

It's summer so we're having cold pink
soup, boiled eggs and warm potatoes.

Recipe for Pink Soup: Shallots, Eggs, Potatoes, Butter
Milk, Beets, Dill, Salt.

After breakfast I head to my parents ceramic studio to make a *Change Token*. It’s moulded from a rare clay mined in our backyard.

The studio is hot, dusty and smells of
dark chocolate and oranges.

It's my favourite place to be and some of my best memories
have their home here.

I once found a nest of newborn rabbits behind the kiln. They
were the size of gumballs, with squinty eyes and folded ears.
I looked after them until they were old enough to hop outside
and into our garden.

Another time, during a thunderstorm, I watched two giant
huntsman spiders dance on the ceiling.

Unexpectedly, a bolt of lightning struck the studio's chimney
and one of the spiders fell into my cup of green tea.

I still drank it.

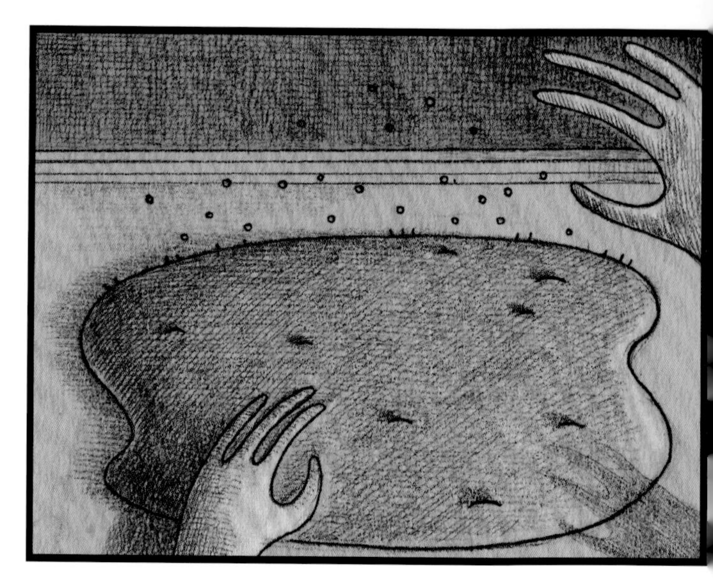

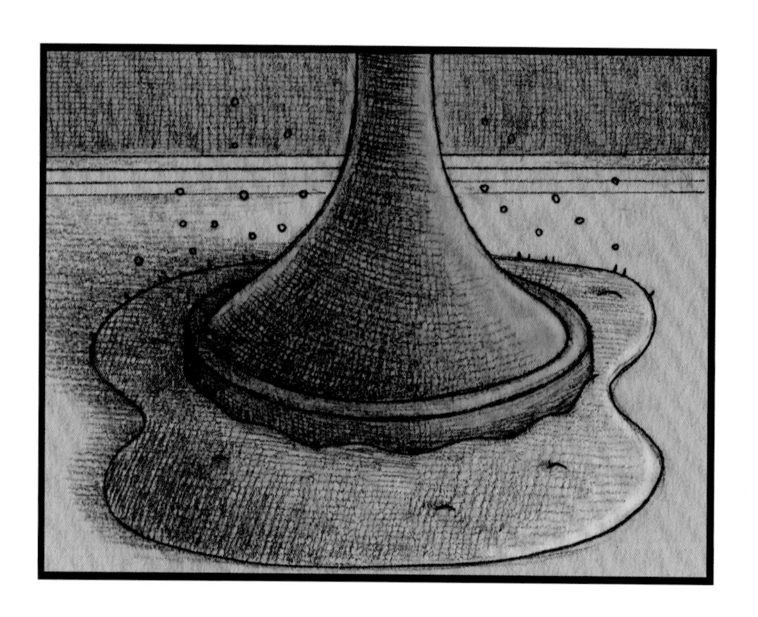

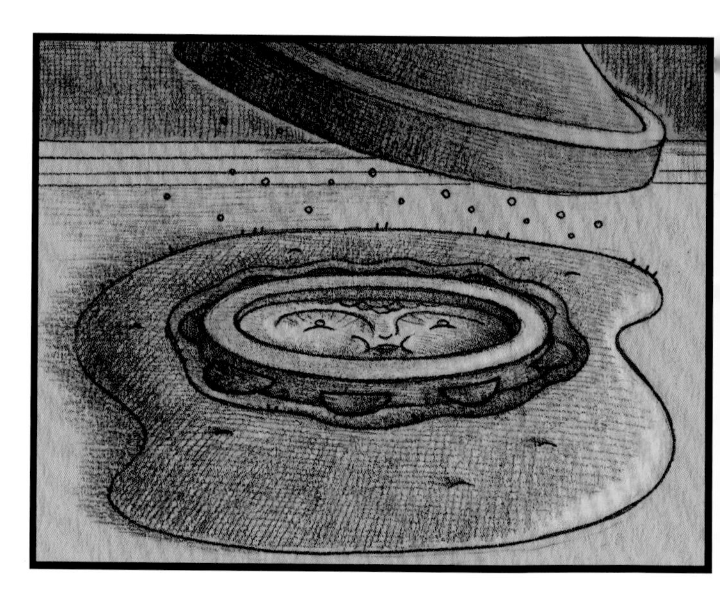

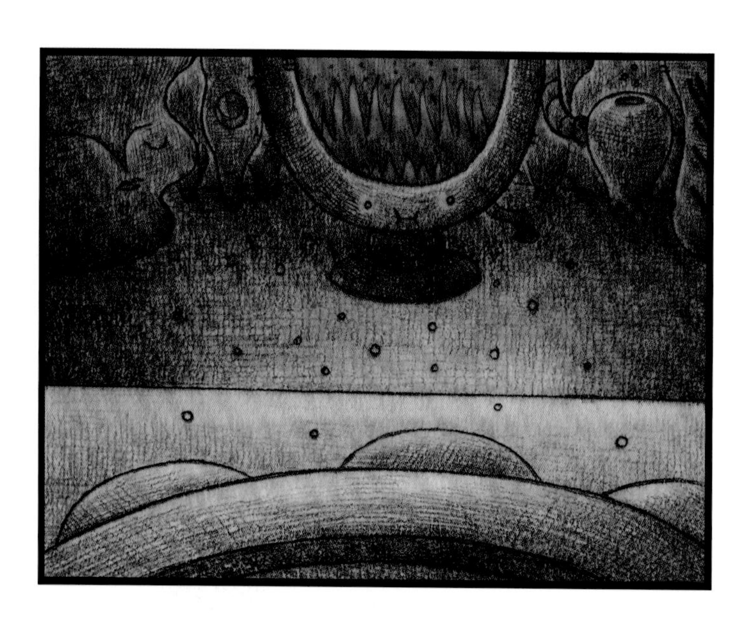

The token's form is made from an ancient metal seal carefully passed down from generations of *Face Changers*. It cools quickly after it's baked and ready for the journey.

According to my sister it takes ten thousand footsteps
to reach the mountain from our house.

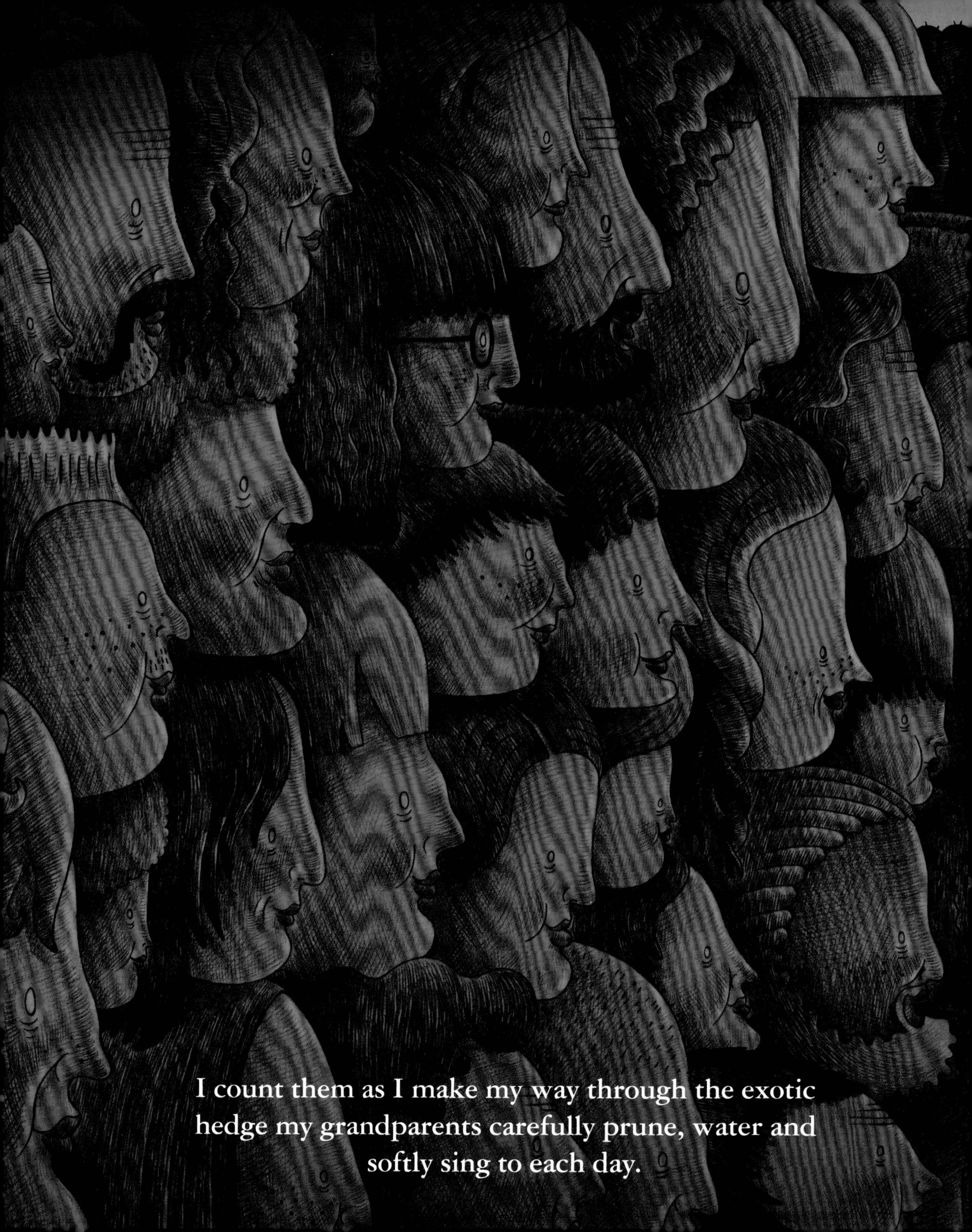
I count them as I make my way through the exotic hedge my grandparents carefully prune, water and softly sing to each day.

1,000...

4,000...

9,000...

10,280.

My sister's legs are longer than mine
so it takes more steps to reach my destination.

I'm finally here!

The inside of the mountain looks a lot bigger than my parent's diagrams, which I'd examined closely for the past few months.

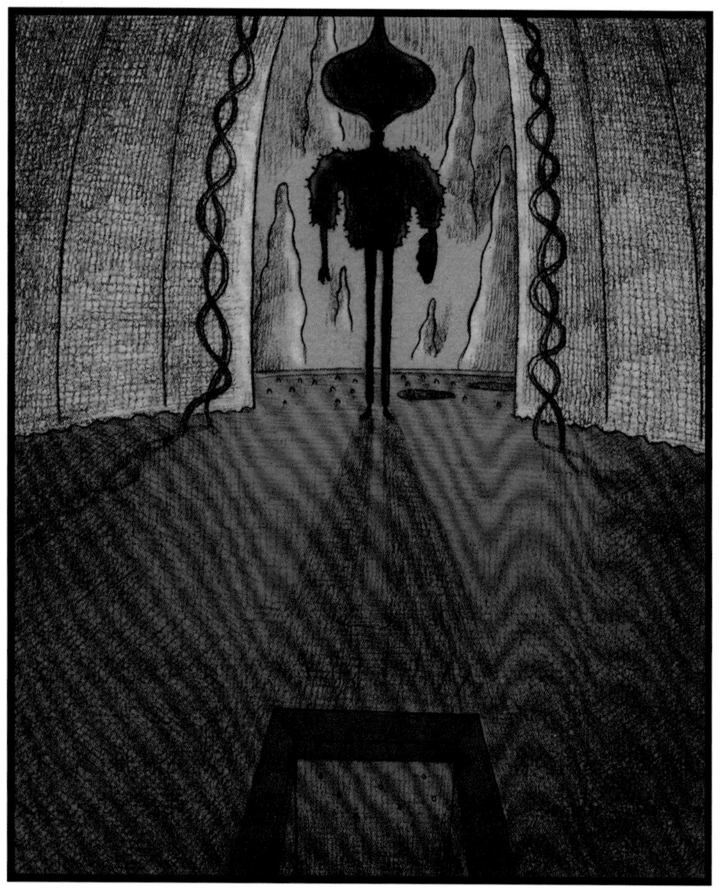

“Don’t lose the token” my sister would repeat on a daily basis.

One year my grandfather dropped the token before inserting it into the mountain’s *Operating Slot*. It rolled down a drain and was swallowed by a slimy fish with needle-like whiskers.

There was no transformation that year.

After the token disappears I visualize it being caught
by a serene hot air balloon,

past congregations of laughing stalagmites

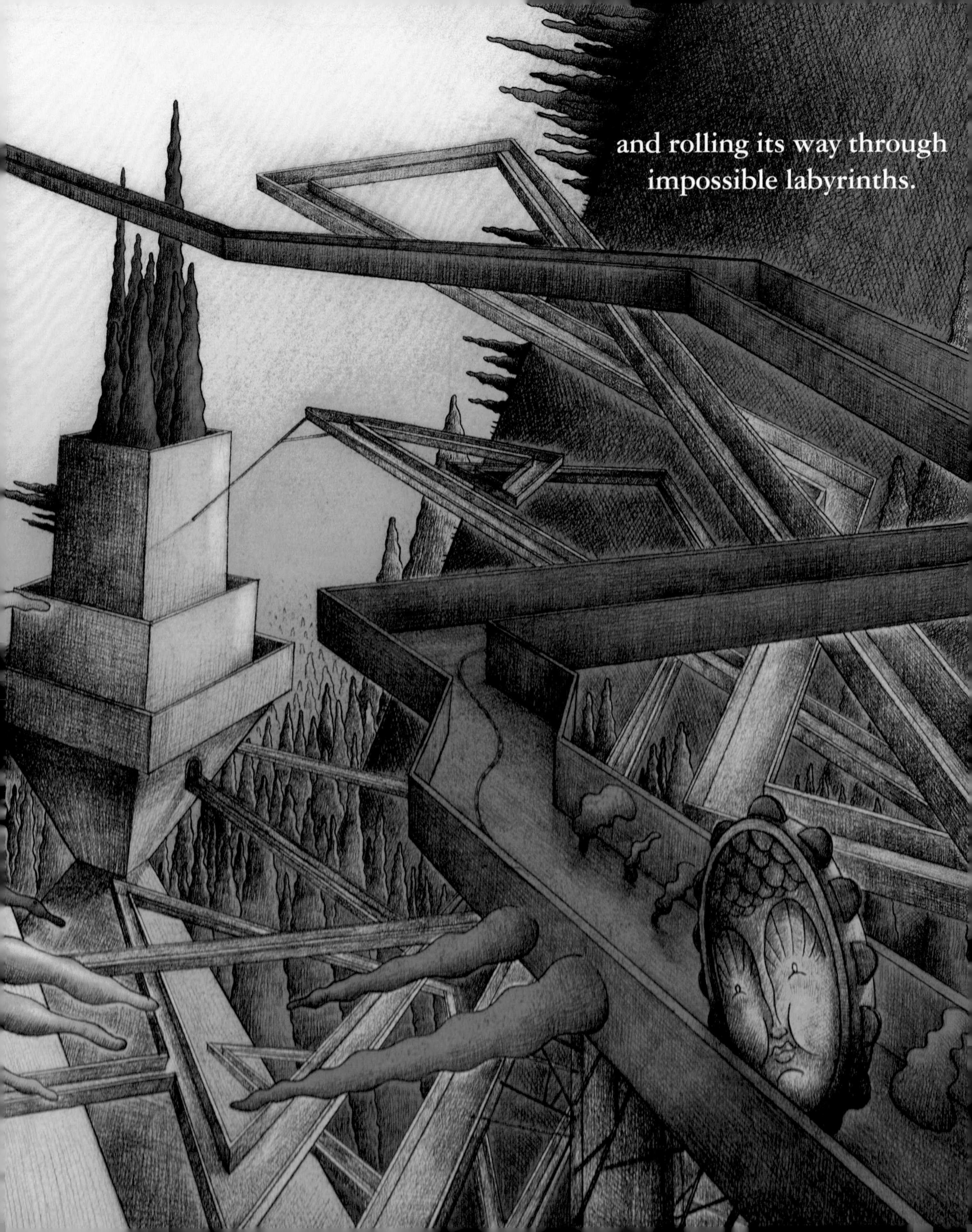
and rolling its way through
impossible labyrinths.

But for all I know it may just vanish into thin air
when it descends into the craggy depths.

I wait for almost thirty minutes and then get a tingling sensation in my stomach—the one you get when something fantastic is about to happen.

In the distance the West Mountain whistles, indicating it's time for the East Mountain to activate.

A sound like a metal lid slowly turning on an empty glass jar emits from deep below me. I've heard this sound from the foothills near my house, but up close I can feel the vibrations.

Then it happens.

The inner workings of the mountain are revealed, pulsating and twirling, ready to create change.

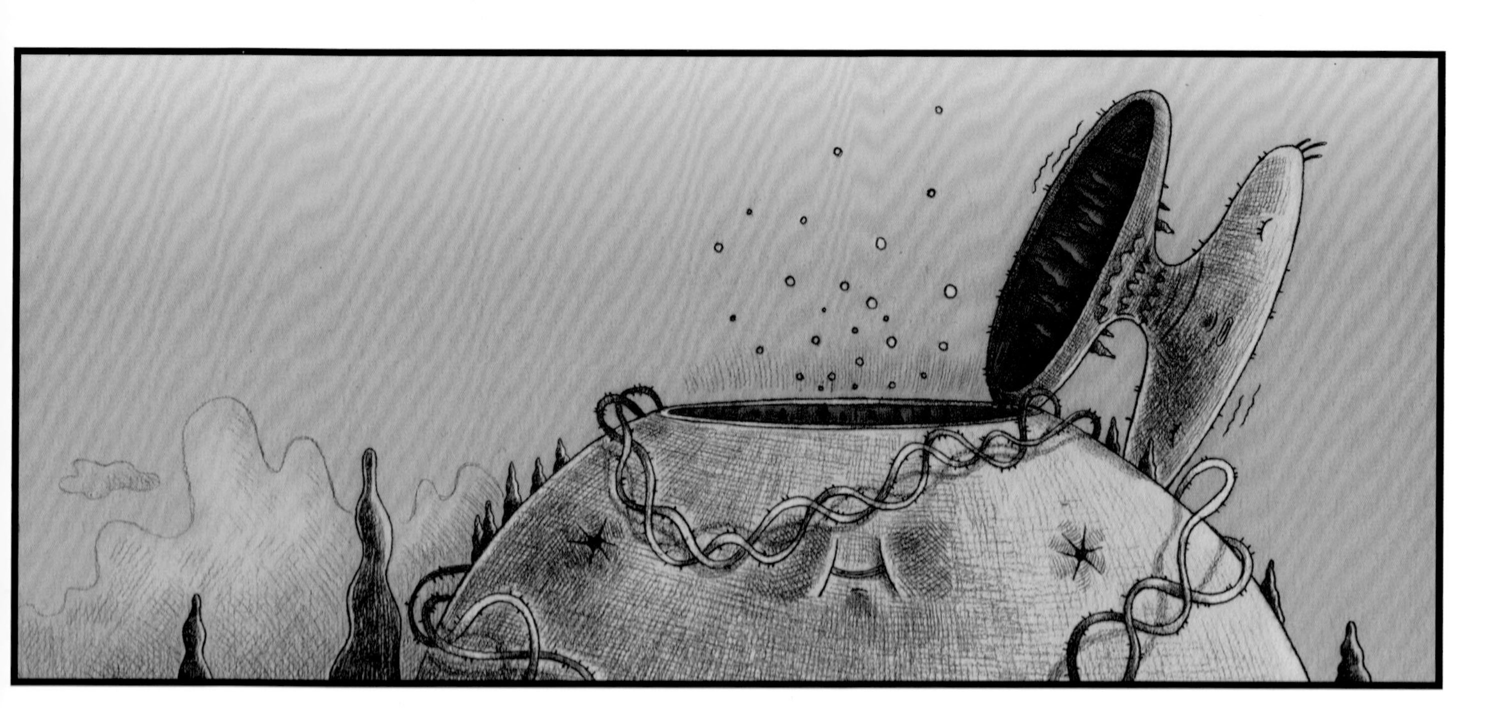

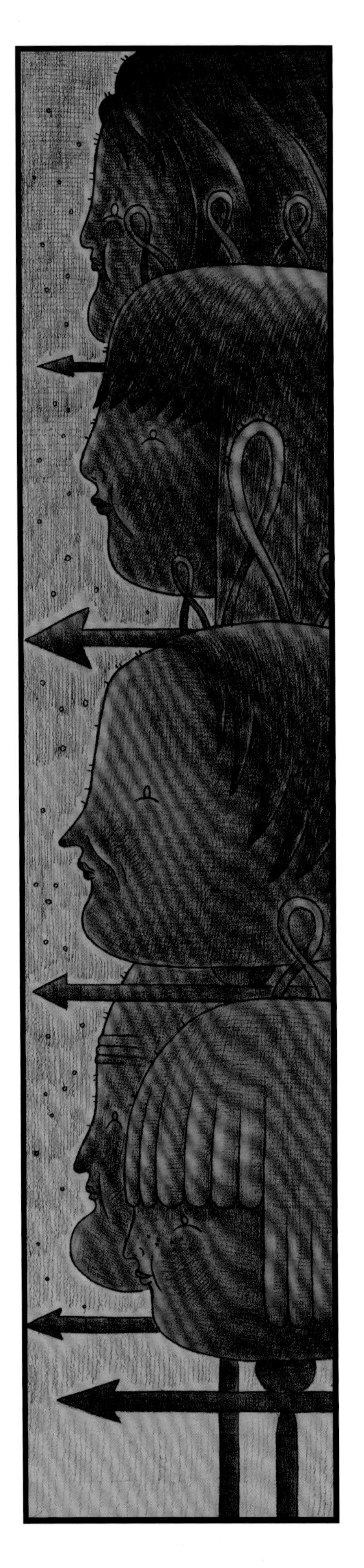

The first puffs of east wind begin to blow and gradually increase until the entire town is engulfed with a steady breeze.

I begin to wonder what my friends and family will look like
now that the transformation is complete.
I think my sister will be something amazing—she always is.

I can sense my own face morphing and taking shape.

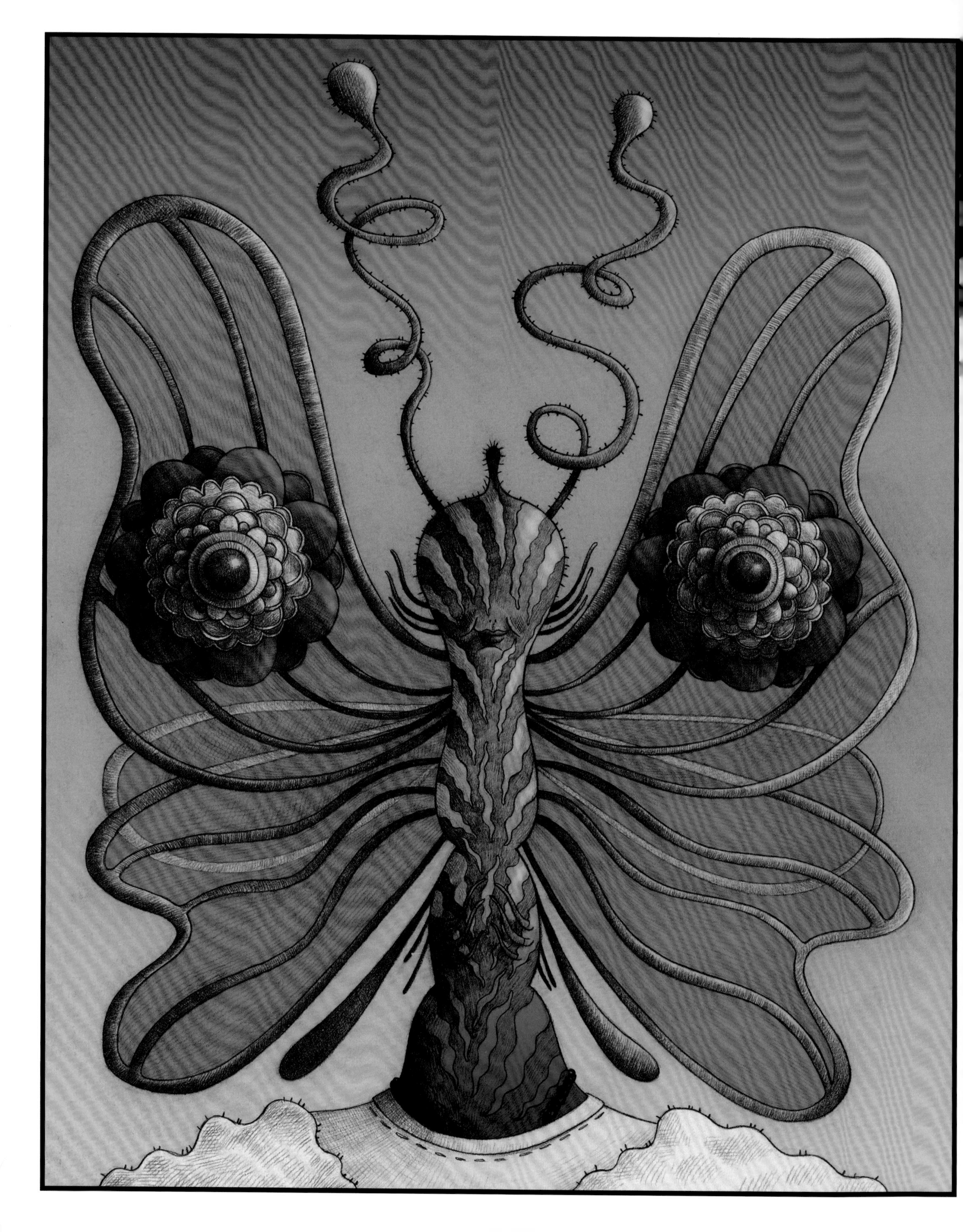

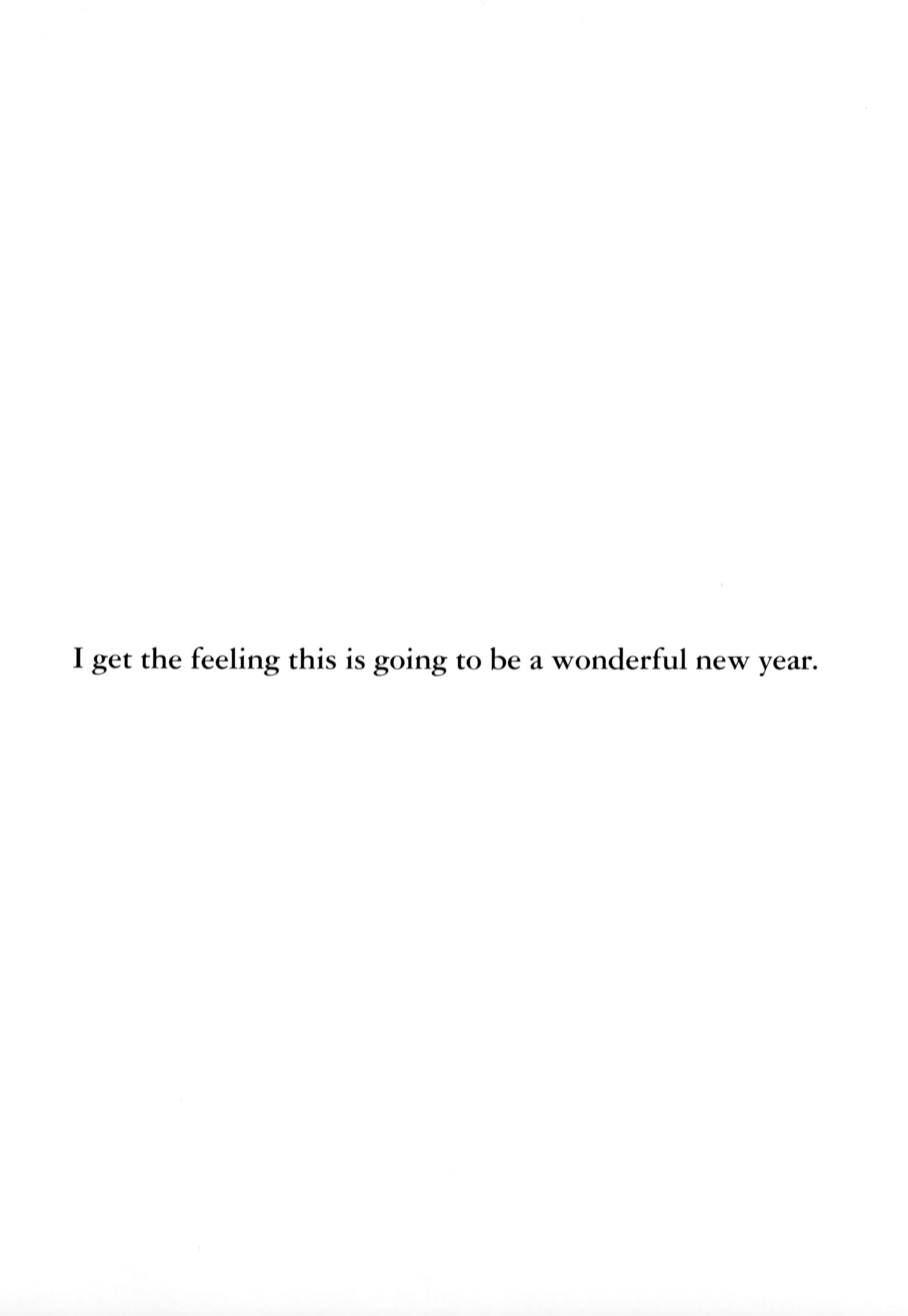

I get the feeling this is going to be a wonderful new year.

thank you

Annie Koyama
Ed Kanerva
Jim Woodring
Helen Koyama
Tristan Müller-Knapp
Steve Alexander
Mum and Dad
Luke Jurevicius
Amber Heeney
Milo, Arkie and Sass Jurevicius
Steve Cober
Andrea Kang
Manale